Milly and Molly

For my grandchildren
Thomas, Harry, Ella and Madeleine

Part of the proceeds from the sale of this book go to 'The Friends of Milly, Molly Inc., a charity which aims to promote the acceptance of diversity and the learning of life skills through literacy - 'for every child, a book.'

Milly, Molly and the Sunhat

Copyright © MM House Publishing, 2002

Gill Pittar and Cris Morrell assert the moral right to be recognised as the author and illustrator of this work.

Published by
MM House Publishing
P O Box 539
Gisborne, New Zealand
email: books@millymolly.com

Printed by Rhythm Consolidated Berhad, Malaysia

ISBN: 1-86972-032-6

10   9   8   7   6   5   4   3   2   1

Milly, Molly
and the
Sunhat

"We may look different
but we feel the same."

It was summer again.
Milly and Molly had just finished their
picnic when a big, brown, straw sunhat
blew along the beach towards them.

"I wonder who owns it?" said Milly.

"Come on, let's find out," suggested Molly.

They didn't need to ask the two boys
digging bunkers in the sand. They could
just see the tops of their sunhats.
It wasn't theirs.

They didn't need to ask the fisherman
sitting on a rock. He had his hat pulled
tightly down over his ears. It wasn't his.

They didn't need to ask the lady filling her
basket with seaweed. She had her hand
firmly on the top of her hat. It wasn't hers.

They didn't need to ask the little girls
building castles in the sand. They had their
hats tied under their chins. It wasn't theirs.

They didn't need to ask the sunbathers
with busy feet. They were under a striped
umbrella. It couldn't be theirs.

They didn't need to ask the old man with
a knobbly stick. He had wild hair escaping
from under his beanie. It wasn't his.

They didn't need to ask the windsurfers.
They had zinc on their noses and wind
in their ears. It wouldn't be theirs.

But what about the four snorklers?
There were four pairs of boots but
only three sunhats!

19

Milly and Molly slipped the big,
brown, straw sunhat under the fourth
pair of boots and ran all the way
back to their picnic basket.

They passed lots of people
on the way home, some with sunhats
and some without.
"I hope we found the right owner,"
said Milly.

"Look," cried Molly. "We did."

Milly, Molly and the Sunhat

The value implicitly expressed in this story is 'honesty' - truthfulness; not lying, cheating or stealing.

When Milly and Molly find a sunhat on the beach they choose to be honest and find the owner.

"We may look different but we feel the same."

MM House

PUBLISHING

Other picture books in the Milly, Molly series include:

- Milly, Molly and Betelgeuse   ISBN 1-86972-011-3

- Milly, Molly and Jimmy's Seeds   ISBN 1-86972-007-5

- Milly, Molly and Oink   ISBN 1-86972-009-1

- Milly, Molly and Pet Day   ISBN 1-86972-010-5

- Milly, Molly and Taffy Bogle   ISBN 1-86972-008-3

- Milly, Molly and the Tree Hut   ISBN 1-86972-013-X

- Milly, Molly and Beefy   ISBN 1-86972-012-1

- Milly and Molly Go Camping   ISBN 1-86972-025-3

- Milly, Molly and Aunt Maude   ISBN 1-86972-033-4

- Milly, Molly and Alf   ISBN 1-86972-022-9

- Milly, Molly and Different Dads   ISBN 1-86972-021-0